Thor

The lightning cracks and the thunder roars

Can you feel the power of mighty Thor?

Upon his chariot he rides the sky

Until the day he is fated to die

But with Mjolnir gripped tight in his hand

The thunderer shall make his final stand

Though nine steps is all he will take

Felled by the venomous world snake

For even the mightiest amongst us all

Will eventually one day fall

Sunna

Sunna carries the sun over high

Letting it burn warmly in the sky

By Allsvinn and Arvak her noble steeds

To shine light upon all is her deed

But Skoll the wolf ever bites at their feet

Come Ragnarok it will be their defeat

So bathe in her warm embrace

While still able they give chase

For when the twilight of the gods arrives

From her warmth and light all will be deprived

Goddesses of Fate

Of man's fate their webs ever spun

Secrets meant for no man's tongue

Urdr spins for the paths past travelled

For mysteries of days yet unravelled

Verdandi for the paths now walked

So to reveal the door to be knocked

And Skuld for the paths now trodden

But forget not that which has been forgotten

Three they are goddesses of fate

To know ones destiny all but one waits

Sif

Fields of gold as far as the eye can see

No greater beauty could there be

Lands blessed by the goddess Sif

An offering of the harvest from our kith

So that we might repay the great goddess

For her work and our lands she does bless

Hel

Within her realm Hel oversees

Her world is death where most will be

A land where the dead still live on

So they drink and sing their songs

Though many have travelled to this place

Only those permitted may have her grace

Heimdall

Born from nine mothers nothing misses his gaze

Vigilant he stands until the Bifrost is ablaze

His ears can hear all across the nine worlds

And eyes that see all that does unfurl

With the sounding of Gjallarhorn it marks the end

Though his honour and strength never will it bend

His fate ultimately is to kill and be killed

At the hands of Loki his blood will be spilled

Frigga

Frigga she is mother to all

Under her gaze families stand tall

For she is the goddess of hearth

By her hands many give birth

Queen is she that dwells in Asgard

Watching over our families on Midgard

Freyja

Within her hall of Folkvangur does she sit

Our fallen heroes gather by her fires now lit

As brisingamen hangs around her slender neck

For her gifts at magic all the gods would trek

Daughter of Njord and brother to Freyr

To the aesir Freyja brought the art of sedir

She chooses from amongst the warriors slain

The goddess whose beauty shall never wane

Loki

Loki is he god of mischief

His words may cause some disbelief

The trickster is what he is called

And by his deeds many are appalled

Though with the help of some pressure applied

He may help or hinder to save his hide

So be wary when dealing with chaos

For his path you may wish to uncross

Skadi

Daughter of Thiassi for vengeance does come

Upon the gates of Asgard does Skadi drum

Her anger though eventually is stayed

A choice of husband for her is to be made

She makes her choice from their feet alone

With their faces hidden and unknown

Njord is chosen though she hoped for another

Though at his gaze she does not shudder

Baldur

The shining one for him do they call

Though by his brother's hand he will fall

Hodr though deceived was he

The point from mistletoe was all it be

Though now pierced his brothers' heart

His hand by Loki guided in the dark

Baldurs death does Vali avenge

The blind god slain now signals the end

Odin

Many names does this wanderer go by

Upon Slleipnir's back he races across the sky

He who sacrificed himself for knowledge unknown

The twilight of the gods he seeks to postpone

A god of war but also of wisdom

Dwelling within Asgard his mighty kingdom

Mani

Swiftly he rides through the night sky

Pulling the moon behind as he flies

Ever chased is he by Hati the wolf

For come Ragnarok he will be engulfed

Brother to Sunna goddess of the sun

Both shall fall when Ragnarok does come

Njord

His home by the shore is where he will be found

As to the ocean his heart is eternally bound

For Njord is god of both the wind and sea

Before we board to him we will beseech

For calm amongst the waves and wind in our sails

Look out towards to sea for him we do hail

Bragi

The god of music and poetry is he

For without him less joy there would be

With runes carved upon his tongue

Magic is found amongst his song

Renowned is he for his wealth of wisdom

His words shall be heard throughout the kingdom

Tyr

For victory in battle Tyr we do invoke

To break his laws wrath you will provoke

Under his watch judgement shall be passed

So that honour and justice may yet still last

Across the world his laws govern the land

To bind the great wolf he freely gave his hand

For none is more honourable than mighty Tyr

Both gods and men his laws they must adhere

Of Aegir and Ran

Within their hall beneath the sea

Ran and Aegir married they be

Together with their nine daughters

Who make up the mighty waters

Ran casts her terrible net

For which many sailors a doom is met

Aegir is a gracious host

Though in his hall you would not boast

Eir

Upon Lyfjaberg her hill of healing

Is where you'll find this goddess treating

From her powers many will recover

Eir is she friend to the all mother

A goddess of healing who lives within Asgard

Though her powers we beseech here in Midgard

The beginning of all

At the beginning there was just the abyss

Ice and fire together they hissed

A chaos of perfect silence once reigned

One that was not meant to be maintained

Between the eternal fires of Muspelheim

And the freezing ice of Niflheim

From the drops of ice Ymir was spawned

With the cow Audhumla a new age dawned

The first of the gods Buri came forth

And thus the giants and gods fought henceforth

Until Ymir by the three sons of Bor was slain

And from his body Midgard was made

The Creation of Midgard

This land from Ymir's remains was made

In which our ancestors bones are laid

The giants flesh was made into the land

Upon which are feet do now stand

His blood became the vast open ocean

On which our boats sail upon its motion

The mountains fashioned from his bones

In which are buried mysterious still unknown

From his teeth the cliffs were forged

Against which the waves crashed and roared

With his hair the first trees are now made

With their beauty and splendour now displayed

His brains blown across the world to form the clouds

Under which we gather to sing our songs out loud

Tongue of Mischief

Ratatoskr with his tongue of mischief

Upon Yggdrasil his words carry disbelief

To Nidhoggr the dragon which coils below

His message in which hate is bestowed

To Verdfolnir the eagle that sits above

His words carry on devoid of love

For Rataoskr has sown his seeds

Destruction of Yggdrasil will be his deed

So trust not in those who carry ill will

As those who do their tongues must still

Ask and Embla

Lifeless trunks found upon the shore

Given life be the three sons of Bor

The breath of life given by Odin's breath

So they live until their death

From Vili he gave the power to understand

So that their wisdom they might expand

And Ve the sense and their outward appearance

As from life's hardships come perseverance

The Golden Apples

Upon the golden apples they feast

In their attempt to best the beast

For old age and time are the foes of all

Even the gods can merely stall

So our time we must use well

For the stories our children will tell

To use out life for something more

Is a song that all can applaud

Mimir's Well

In this path we all must walk

More should we do than just talk

Now place your eye in Mimir's well

To unveil the story you will tell

If something there is you will take

Then first you place something at stake

For there is nothing in life

That first comes without sacrifice

The Beauty of Spring

As life begins to bloom once more

And the frozen earth begins to thaw

The beauty of spring comes to life

Marking the end to the winter strife

Beneath the sky life starts its return

As the wheel of time continues to turn

A careful balance between us all

The beauty of Midgard continues to enthral

The Return of Mjolnir

Mighty and proud the thunderer stands tall

Against the giant Thrymr he will brawl

Stolen at night and hidden away

But now Thor's temper he must stay

For the return of Mjolnir a price is set

Frejya's hand and no single threat

The goddess of beauty though rejects

So Loki the trickster a plan he injects

Deceit and cunning all in his stride

So now the mighty must cast of their pride

Disguised as Frejya goddess of beauty

Reclaiming his hammer is his duty

Thrymr blinded by love and eager to wed

A mistake that will cost Thrymr's head

A Sacrifice of Himself to Thee

For nine days he hung there

In his side he plunged his spear

For nine nights upon the great tree

A sacrifice of himself to thee

The secret knowledge of runes he seeks

Gifted to man for all to speak

Knowledge and wisdom now passed along

For us all to join in his song

In Search of Glory

As we wonder far and wide

Looking to the gods to be our guide

In search of glory do we tread

Our enemies will feel such dread

With our wooden dragons we sail

To honour the gods which we hail

As our deeds shall not ring hollow

For destiny awaits those who follow

Kith and Kin

From friends of old and friends anew

Gathered together as we step through

We drink to our bonds of kith and kin

And to the gods of which we still sing

The memories we have made here today

Forever in our minds shall they stay

So may our joy and health forever last

And our hardships to quickly past

The contest

Brokkr and Eitri the master smiths

Tricked by Loki into forging gifts

The sons of Ivaldi against they are pit

Two families forges with fires now lit

Each to present three gifts to the gods

With Loki playing each at odds

A contest which the gods will choose

Though a trick played by Loki could cause them to lose

A trick that causes them a major error

Which ultimately could cost them their wager

But the gods see past their small flaw

And see the fruits which their labour bore

Wild and Free

The mighty bear roams wild and free

Within his forest he will oversee

Between the trees and beneath the sky

In the shade he watches them fly

Sitting patiently for his time to strike

For under his sky he knows no plight

Within his realm there is a peace

One that will last long after he's deceased

Fenrir

Under the stars the great wolf lies

Until the day the gods will die

Tricked by those he trusted the most

For his strength though he did boost

Another path he might have walked

Instead of the dark in which he stalks

One moment and perhaps all would change

Instead he's left with a feeling so strange

With anger and hate growing inside

But soon his vengeance and Odin will die

Loki is Bound

For his hand in Baldur's death

Loki will be punished until his last breath

Above his head a venomous snake is placed

Now the god of mischief is eternally disgraced

Bound to a rock by the innards of his son

By all but his wife now him they shun

There in anguish he is to remain

Until the time comes where the gods will be slain

The scorching of Beauty

Three times did they burn her

Scorching the beauty of Frejya

Three times did she come again

Blamed for the folly of men

Anger and hate begins to grow

From the seeds they did sow

So now both sides march to war

Aesir and Vanir drench the floor

Until the day they sought respite

Now the see a better path in sight

The Road to Hel

For nine nights along the paths he sped

Until he reached the realm of the dead

Past the black woods were sharp are their leaves

Until the gates of Hel he does reach

Though barred is the way to the corpse shore

So through the sky does Sleipnir soar

Faced is Hermod with an impossible task

Bauldr's release from her realm he did ask

If all beings shall weep for the shining one

The goddess Hel shall let his task be done

Though a trick played by the god of mischief

Will eventually prevent Baldur's release

Yggdrasil

Nine worlds held by the great world tree

Near its roots you'll find the spinster three

The Bifrost connects together the worlds

Still hiding its mysteries for us to unfurl

Many a beast call Yggdrasil their home

Upon the trees branches they do roam

Its beauty and splendour a true sight to behold

Of its greatness the past stories have told

Freyr Shall Fall

To Skirnir does he give his blade

With Gerdr's hand a bride will be made

Though nine nights must Freyr await

For his love which he would state

With rings of gold do the two trade

So loves currents together they could wade

Now armed with just an antler

Freyr shall fall facing mighty Surtur

Hugin and Munin

Every morning across Midgard they have flown

To Odin they bring their news to be shown

Though worries does he that Hugin will not return

For Munin he worries more of news he might learn

His thought and memory do they represent

So out to the world ever are they sent

The twilight of the gods

Sent forth the hordes of Surtur will burn all

And the great Bifrost bridge shall finally fall

The chains that hold Fenrir no more will they bind

For his betrayal the all father he shall find

Jormungandr the great snake shall come forth from the sea

So that against Thor he can meet his destiny

Upon the ship Naglfar do Hel and her legions sail

Against the mighty gods they shall prevail

On the field of Vigrid the einherjar do gather

Against the giant Surtur Freyr stands with but an antler

The black wolf Garm and Tyr each other they will slay

Upon the field of battle the bodies rot and decay

Until the world sinks into the depths of the sea

As once more everything shall cease to be

But again the worlds are to be remade again

Led by the risen Bauldr the gods shall recreate men

Fafnirsbane

Against Odin Hreithmar makes his demand

For the death of his son he did command

Though begrudgingly Hreithmar is paid

Upon his gold a curse is now laid

Upon the sight of his father's treasure

Fafnir killed him for greed and for pleasure

Overtime time a dragon did Fafnir became

Though a hero is found by his brother Reign

To kill his brother Sigurd is now tasked

And to cook the dragons heart he also is asked

Though the dragon now lays slain

The birds sing of the deceit from Reign

With sword in hand Reign too lays dead

So Sigurd keeps the treasure in his stead

Challenges for the Gods

Within this land do the mighty giants thrive

The castle of Utgarda-Loki do the gods arrive

Taunts and boasts spew from his mouth

Angered by this within the giant's house

Utgarda-Loki issues the gods a challenge for each to beat

Loki the trickster is the first to take his seat

His challenge was to eat all which he could see

Against the fire of Logi his lose he does not believe

Next Thjalfi the swift is to take his position

Racing against the thoughts of Hugi with ambition

Though like Loki does poor Thjalfi also fail

Thor steps up and takes his horn a single gulp for him to prevail

Though three he takes but still it does not empty

So the giant allows Thor to show his strength of plenty

To lift the giant's cats' paws from up off the floor

Though he fails for another challenge he does roar

To wrestle anyone willing within the giant's hall

But against the elderly Elli does the might god fall

So for now within these walls shall the gods sleep

For tomorrow they will know of the giants deceit

The Einherjar

Within the hall of Vahalla do the mighty live on

Heroes of old whose deeds carry on in song

The Einherjar feast merrily each night

For the next morning again they will fight

Odin's warriors chosen amongst the slain

Until the coming of Ragnarok they do train

Muspellheim

In the land of eternal fire

Sits a giant with a single desire

Surtur is he ruler of flame

Against Freyr he is his bane

All nine world his legions will burn

Though for now he awaits his turn

Jotunheim

Here in Jotunheim do the giants dwell

It is here that their numbers do swell

A place eternally gripped by winters grasp

Where the warmth of the sun never does last

Within this wild land of ice and snow

Where few travellers shall ever dare to go

Svartalheim

Here is a land though twice is it named

Where many dwell whose work is famed

Sometimes called Svartalheim but by another it goes

Nidavellir where the Dwarven crafts are shown

A place of true subterranean splendour

Where their walls glow from the embers

Niflheim

Within this world of ice and mist

All the roads to one place do twist

Where the well of Hvergelmir is found

From which all rivers too are bound

And where the fearsome Nidhog also dwells

Upon the roots of Yggdrasil his belly does swell

Midgard

Here within this realm which we call home

Upon which our feet now do roam

Gifted to us from the gods themselves

A world which we can make a home for ourselves

Its beauty and wonder written in our song

For deep within our heart nature we still long

Asgard

Home to the mighty Aesir gods of war

Within their hall's weapons are stored

Led by Odin the father of us all

Inside its gates is where be Vahall

Its walls built strong and proud

Though soon a darkness will shroud

Vanahiem

The land which the ancient magic still flows

And where the halls of the Vanir first rose

A realm with fields as far as the eye can see

Home to the ancient gods of magic and fertility

With beauty and splendour found in every corner

And its ancient wisdom awaiting the avid learner

Alfheim

Here is where the elves of light be

This world ruled by the god of fertility

A land filled with such wondrous light

That shines even in the dead of night

The splendour of which is told within our songs

Where the steams of magic flow ever strong

Helheim

The realm of Hel the daughter of Loki

Found beneath the roots of the world tree

Many paths will lead to this ancient world

Where the souls of the dead within still swirl

Within this realm where no light may shine

They patiently await the end of time

Printed in Great Britain
by Amazon